MAKHMALI

AS SOFT AS HEART CAN BE

RAGHVENDRA SAGAR GAUR

"To all the lovers who have had to let go of love and who has **changed** in love, this **story** is for you.

(Yaad rakhna mohabbat ka dusra naam jaane dena hai...)

Remember them, and cherish every memory you shared before you made the difficult decision to let them go for their own happiness. It's never easy to part ways with someone you care about, but sometimes, *letting them go is the greatest act of love you can offer."*

Contents

Acknowledgements   *vii*

BASED ON TRUE...   *ix*

Foreword   *xi*

Preface   *xiii*

BEFORE STARTING   *xv*

    1. THE PLAYER's PLAY   1

    2. THE BOLD ERA   17

    3. THE PLAYER GOT PLAYED   30

    4. AGAIN AND ALWAYS   47

    5. THE LAST OF HER   60

LOVE IS TO LET GO   73

TIME NEVER WAITS   75

THEY WILL BE ALWAYS THERE   77

STORY HAS NOT ENDED   79

WAITED YOUR ENTIRE LIFE   81

IN HER MEMORIES   83

COVER PAGE RELEVENCE   85

EXTRA   87

Thank you   89

Acknowledgements

Special thanks to Mridul Mohanta, my brother from another mother, for his efforts in designing the cover page of this book (template from PIXABY). His creativity, dedication, and boundless support have brought this vision to life in a way that words cannot express. Thank you for being a part of this journey, for your society friendship, and yes... "Meri jaan hai tu (Stefan to my Damon).

Special thanks to AI tools for helping me fix the errors, as I'm not a writer but a storyteller. Thank you for being a part of this journey, for your Net friendship, and yes... "Mera ROBOT hai tu (Chitti to my Vaseegaran)."

Based On True...

A special thanks to my two friends, from whom I have loosely adapted the school life of one close friend and the girl he deeply loves (Viyaan and Viyaara). Your experiences and stories have inspired this narrative, and I am grateful for the memories you've shared with me."

The rest of the story is a work of fiction. Any resemblance to real events, people, or places is purely coincidental and unintentional.

Foreword

Special thanks to all my friends who have read the first raw draft and provided invaluable feedback. Your encouragement, insights, and unwavering support have been instrumental in shaping this story. It is because of you that this book exists today, and I am truly grateful for your time and dedication.

Thank you for believing in this journey and for helping me bring my vision to life.

Preface

I am a 23-year-old engineer by profession. I'm not a writer but a storyteller who likes to create stories. My journey into the world of writing began as a way to express the emotions and stories that are in my head, as well as my undying love for CINEMA. In this journey, I found inspiration through my friends—through the films and life lessons of Shah Rukh Khan (Huge FAN), whose portrayal of love, sacrifice, and selflessness in movies profoundly shaped my understanding of relationships.

One lesson from his work resonates deeply with me: the idea that true love is not about holding on but about letting go. This story is a reflection of that very lesson.

This book is not just a narrative; it is a tribute to all those who have loved deeply, only to learn that sometimes, love means setting someone free.

Thank you for taking the time to read this story. I hope it resonates with you as deeply as it has with me.

AND PLEASE READ THE BOOK TILL THE LAST PAGE.

Before Starting

I always thought of this story as a **MOVIE** and never as a **BOOK**. Sorry for any mistakes I made in this book. Now, let's dive into the world of MAKHMALI...

CHAPTER ONE

THE PLAYER'S PLAY

In life, there are many different kinds of people, studs, nerds, shy individuals, and so on. Each person has their unique qualities that set them apart from the rest. However, when you have it all, it's something truly special. Imagine being the person who not only excels academically but also shines in sports, and is adored by everyone around you.

The best part of all this is when girls admire you, you stand out in sports, and you're also a school topper. This combination is rare, but for some, it's the perfect mix of talent, charm, and charisma. In Viyaan's case, it was exactly this combination that made him a standout student in his school.

His reputation for being talented and charming made him a natural leader. He was admired by his peers and respected by everyone around him. With every achievement, he grew more confident and established himself as someone people looked up to. His ability to balance academics and extracurricular activities effortlessly was something that set him apart.

Viyaan's presence in the school wasn't just noticed, it was celebrated. He didn't just get through school life; he owned it. He was at the top in nearly everything he did, making him someone others aspired to be like. His peers admired his ease, his skill, and his ability to be both brilliant and likable.

In this chapter of his life, Viyaan had already become famous in school. He was fully prepared to take on the world, ready for whatever came next. But to truly understand how he reached that level of success, we need to rewind.

We have to look back at the journey that led him to where he was now, to when he was just beginning to make his mark. It wasn't always easy, and it didn't happen overnight. To truly understand the essence of who Viyaan had become, we need to explore the steps he took, the challenges he faced, and how he made his way to the top.

Let's go back in time, **four years ago**, when Viyaan was an ambitious student with big dreams. He was already good in school and sports, but there was something else that made him stand out. Viyaan loved being creative, and he wanted to make his school life even more exciting.

He wasn't just happy with being good at studies and sports. He wanted to do something special that would bring his friends together and make school more fun. He decided to create something no one had expected, a board game that could bring everyone together and make them enjoy playing and working as a team.

It was around the time of the school festival, an event everyone looked forward to. Every year, there were sports, music, dance, and debates, but Viyaan felt like something was missing. He wanted to create an activity that would be different and fun for everyone, not just something that showcased individual talent.

That's when he had the idea: a board game. Viyaan wanted to create a game that everyone could enjoy, one that would be fun and exciting. He remembered a game he loved as a child, but he wanted to make it even better, with more fun and challenges. His goal was to bring his friends together and make the game something everyone could enjoy.

Viyaan worked hard on creating the game. He spent a lot of time thinking about the rules, designing the board, and making it as fun as possible. He didn't just want it to be about playing, it had to be an experience that everyone would enjoy together.

Viyaan got his closest friends to test the game first. They gave him their ideas and suggestions. He made many changes to the game until it felt just right. As he worked, more and more of his friends got excited to try it out. Soon, everyone was talking about the game.

Finally, the day of the school festival came, and Viyaan was ready. He set up a booth where students could come and play his game. The festival was full of energy, and many students were curious to try the game. It was a big hit! Everyone had fun playing together, laughing, and enjoying the game.

His game became the highlight of the festival. People loved how it brought everyone together. Viyaan felt proud. He didn't just want to win in school, he wanted to create something that would make people smile and build memories together. And he had done just that.

After the festival, students kept talking about Viyaan's game. It wasn't just the game itself that people remembered, but how it brought them closer and made them work together. Viyaan felt happy because he had created something that helped his friends bond and have fun.

This experience was important for Viyaan. He realized that true success wasn't just about being the best at school or sports. It was about using your talents to make a positive impact on others. The board game was just the beginning, and Viyaan knew there were many more adventures to come.

At this point in his life, Viyaan had friends both in the classroom and in his neighborhood. He was well-liked by many, but there were a few people who truly understood him and supported his creative ideas. These were the people who stuck by his side through thick and thin. Viyaan's circle of close friends was small but tight-knit, and they shared in his excitement when he introduced the board game to them.

As more and more students played the game, Viyaan's reputation grew. People started to see him not just as a smart student or athlete, but also as a creator and innovator. His ability to take a simple idea and turn it into something fun and exciting made him stand out even more.

His influence in school grew, and everyone wanted to be a part of what he had started. Viyaan had built something that united people and brought them together, and that made him even more respected among his peers.

The board game became a regular part of school life. Students played it during breaks, after school, and even on weekends. It became something everyone looked forward to, and it was clear that Viyaan had made a lasting impact. His simple idea had turned into something that brought joy to many, and he couldn't be more happy with the result.

What started as a small project had now become a big part of school culture, and Viyaan had proven that with creativity and passion, you could turn anything into something truly amazing.

But Viyaan's talent didn't stop there. In addition to his academic prowess and his creative streak, he was also an athlete. He played football with great skill, and his natural athleticism made him a standout player on the school team.

Football was something that he loved, a sport that allowed him to express himself in ways that academics couldn't. On the field, Viyaan was a force to be reckoned with. His speed, agility, and team spirit made him a key player, and he helped his school's team win numerous matches, further cementing his reputation as someone who excelled in every area of life.

It was a balance of academic success, creativity, and athletic achievement that set him apart from his peers.

Despite all of this, what truly made Viyaan special was his ability to connect with others. He had a rare gift of being able to get along with everyone, whether they were his friends, classmates, or even teachers. He made an effort to be kind to everyone, to listen when others needed someone to talk to, and to always bring positivity to the table.

His easygoing nature and willingness to help others made him well-liked by all, and it was this combination of qualities that made him the kind of person people wanted to be around. It wasn't just his good looks or his athletic abilities that made him popular, it was his genuine personality and his ability to make everyone feel valued.

Now, as a COLLEGE student, much has changed for Viyaan. He's grown, learned new things, and faced challenges that have helped him become even more confident and determined. But when he looks back at those four years in school, he sees a journey filled with memories of friendship, creativity, and success.

And the board game? It remains one of his proudest achievements from that time, a reminder of how something as simple as an idea can bring people together and create lasting bonds. Viyaan may be in college now, but his school days, filled with adventure, fun, and triumph, will always be a cherished part of his story.

4 years back, Viyaan's team was in a tough spot. They were trailing by a score of 2-1, and there was little time left on the clock. Viyaan's heart was racing as he knew this could be his last chance to make a difference. He could feel the weight of the game pressing on him, the hopes of his teammates resting on his shoulders. He was determined not to let them down.

His best friend, seeing the desperation in his eyes, passed him the ball. Without hesitation, Viyaan took control, his feet moving swiftly as he dribbled the ball past several defenders, heading straight for the goalkeeper. He could see the opening in the defense, a small gap between the goalkeeper's position and the post. It was now or never.

With a deep breath, Viyaan took the shot, sending the ball flying toward the goal with precision and power. Time seemed to slow down as the ball hurtled toward its target. But in a split second, the goalkeeper lunged and made a spectacular save, diving to his right and stopping the ball just inches from the net.

The crowd let out a collective groan of disappointment as the whistle blew, signaling the end of the match. Despite Viyaan's incredible effort, his team had lost.

The defeat stung, but it didn't stop his friends who came rushing to him with enthusiasm. They surrounded him, clapping him on the back and offering words of encouragement. Viyaan was one of those rare person who could make friends wherever he went, and in moments like this, it was clear how much his team admired him, not just for his skills on the field, but for his leadership and sportsmanship.

Amid the congratulatory cheers, Inaaya, Viyaan's girlfriend, approached him with a warm smile. She wrapped her arms around him in a comforting hug, and whispered, "Well done." Her words meant more to him than anyone could understand, and they helped ease the sting of the loss.

Inaaya was different from the other girls in Viyaan's life. She was the last person in his circle whom he hadn't dated, yet despite their close friendship, Viyaan had never pursued anything romantic with her. They shared a unique bond, and it was clear that there was a special connection between them.

Inaaya was a young woman from Delhi, with a passion for dance and a strong commitment to physical fitness. She was talented, confident, and driven, much like Viyaan, and over time, her affection for him had grown.

At first, Inaaya had been hesitant to get involved with Viyaan. She had seen him date several girls in their group and break up with them for various reasons. To her, it seemed like he was just another player in the game of romance, someone who moved on quickly. She wasn't sure she wanted to be just another name on his list of short-lived relationships.

But, as they say, you can't ignore the best in the group. Despite her reservations, Inaaya eventually found herself drawn to him.

She began to see a side of Viyaan that others didn't, the thoughtful, kind, and genuine side that had always been hidden beneath his charm and popularity. It was then that she decided to give him a chance, and they started dating.

Their relationship was anything but ordinary. Viyaan was known for his charisma and his ability to make friends with just about anyone, but with Inaaya, he felt a sense of comfort and understanding that he hadn't experienced with anyone else.

Viyaan found himself looking forward to the moments they spent together, whether they were studying, going for walks, or simply chatting about life. He had never been one to shy away from challenges, but Inaaya was a challenge in her own right, someone who didn't settle for anything less than the best. And that made him respect her even more.

One day, Inaaya asked Viyaan to skip class with her. Viyaan, never one to turn down a chance to spend time with her, agreed without hesitation. He had always found it easy to give in to her requests; there was something about her that made him want to do anything for her.

They spent the day together, enjoying each other's company, and when it was time for him to return to school, he went to his final lesson and then headed home. His parents were always proud of him, after all, he was a scholar who excelled in every subject.

They admired his ability to balance his academic responsibilities with his social life and athletic side. Viyaan's success was a reflection of his dedication and hard work, and his parents couldn't have been more pleased with his achievements.

They sat together in the schoolyard one afternoon, basking in the warmth of the sun, Inaaya turned to him with a soft smile. She had always been the type of person to speak her mind, and today was no different.

"I feel like we're incredibly special," she said, her voice filled with sincerity. "Like we're incredibly close, in a way that no one else can understand."

Viyaan felt a rush of emotion as her words resonated deeply within him. They had been through so much together, and yet, it felt like their bond was only growing stronger with time. In that moment, Viyaan knew that no matter what the future held, their relationship would always be something he treasured.

The very next day, after their heartfelt conversation in the schoolyard, Viyaan did the unexpected. He called Inaaya, his tone serious as he apologized. "I'm sorry, Inaaya, but I think we're just not compatible. I don't feel the same anymore." It was a decision that shocked her, and even though Viyaan tried to soften the blow, the hurt was evident in her eyes.

She didn't understand why things had changed so quickly, but despite the breakup, they remained part of the same friend group, and everyone knew what had happened. Life moved on, and Viyaan continued to maintain his usual carefree attitude.

In the following days, Viyaan threw himself into his social life. He was known for being the life of any party, and when he was with his society friends, it was impossible not to notice his presence. He was often seen dancing, laughing, and talking with friends as if the world revolved around him.

His ability to seamlessly move between different groups, whether it was his school friends or his society friends that were part of his charm. He was a social guy, always keeping things exciting and unpredictable.

Despite his popularity, Viyaan was still recovering from his breakup with Inaaya. It had been a tough time for him, and although he appeared to be moving on, there was still a sense of emptiness inside.

Every day after school, he was seen with a different girl, but none of these were serious relationships. Viyaan made it clear to everyone around him that he wasn't looking for anything long-term at the moment. He wasn't ready to dive into a committed relationship again, and he wanted to focus on enjoying his life without the pressure of a serious romance.

Although he wasn't officially dating anyone, there was one girl from his society who had always shown interest in him. She was sweet and attentive, and Viyaan appreciated the attention she gave him. However, he wasn't particularly drawn to her. He valued her friendship but didn't feel the spark that he had with someone like Inaaya.

Viyaan didn't want to lead her on, so he kept things casual. His actions sent mixed signals to those around him, and some people didn't understand where he stood. But for Viyaan, it was clear that he was focused on living in the moment and enjoying life as it came, not rushing into anything serious.

He didn't date a lot of girls after Inaaya, but his reputation for being charming and charismatic meant that many girls were drawn to him. His friends often did his assignments for him, knowing that he had a way with people that made things happen.

Viyaan didn't always have to put in the hard work; his charm and connections were enough to get him through most situations.

But as carefree as Viyaan appeared, there was a mischievous side to him that few knew about. One day, during a break in class, Viyaan found himself feeling bored and looking for a little excitement.

He decided to pull a prank. He sprayed a bottle of perfume on a classmate's desk, just enough to leave a strong scent in the air.

Then, to make matters worse, Viyaan carelessly tossed a matchstick into the mix. The perfume and fire quickly combined, and before long, a small fire had started on the desk.

Panic spread quickly as the teacher rushed to put out the flames. Students looked on in shock, unsure of what to do. In the chaos that followed, Viyaan was able to slip away without anyone noticing he was involved.

Despite the trouble he caused, there were no real consequences for Viyaan. Why? Because he was a star student, always getting grades of 95 percent or higher. His academic excellence was so impressive that it seemed to excuse all his pranks.

After all, how could anyone punish a student who was constantly at the top of his class? Viyaan's reputation for being smart and talented meant that his mischief went unnoticed, and he managed to get away with things others would have been punished for.

It was another example of how his achievements in school worked in his favor, allowing him to keep his fun, mischievous side hidden from most teachers.

Even though Viyaan got away with most of his mischief, his behavior didn't go unnoticed. At a parent-teacher conference, one of his teachers voiced a concern to his mother. "Your son is always roaming around with girls," the teacher remarked. "He never settles down, and he's more interested in socializing than focusing on his studies." Viyaan's mother, always proud of her son's academic achievements, didn't know how to respond.

She had always been supportive of Viyaan, but hearing this complaint made her wonder if there was more to her son's behavior than met the eye. She wasn't sure how to handle it, and the issue caused a bit of tension at home. Viyaan's parents wanted him to be responsible, but they also knew he was excelling in his studies, and that made it difficult to criticize him too harshly.

Viyaan continued living life his way, enjoying the freedom he had earned through his accomplishments. He seemed to have it all figured out. But deep down, there was always a part of him that knew things couldn't stay this way forever.

He was on a path that felt exciting in the moment, but he couldn't help but wonder what the future would hold. For now, though, he was content with living in the present, embracing each new day with a new adventure, surrounded by friends, laughter, and excitement.

Viyaan had always been a free spirit, never one to stay tied down. His unpredictable nature was part of his charm. Despite the fact that his classmates often joked about his dating life, Viyaan was focused on his future, at least for the time being. His current preoccupation, however, was a society-wide cricket match that was going on in his locality, an event that had drawn a lot of attention.

The match began with a surprising twist—the team's star player was dismissed without scoring a single run. This unexpected event left everyone wondering what would happen next, as the team found themselves in a tough spot. The atmosphere was tense, and the pressure was on.

However, when it was Viyaan's turn to bat, he quickly stepped up and proved his worth. He was determined to turn the situation around. The moment he took his position, his confident stance and precise strikes had everyone on the edge of their seats.

Viyaan's bat made contact with the ball, sending it flying through the air. His timing and technique were flawless. In no time, Viyaan had turned the game around, putting his team in a much stronger position.

Though he couldn't seal the victory, his performance was nothing short of heroic. He had given everything he had, refusing to let the team down. His resilience and determination shone through as he took charge in a critical moment.

Once again, Viyaan had proven that, despite his carefree attitude in other areas of his life, he always gave his best when it mattered the most. When it came to the things that truly mattered, Viyaan stepped up with all his strength, showing that he was a true team player and someone who could always be counted on in times of need.

Soon after, the exam season arrived, and Viyaan was faced with the daunting challenge of 11th grade, which was widely regarded as one of the toughest academic years. The pressure was intense, and everyone around him could feel the weight of the workload.

Despite all the stress and expectations, Viyaan made a bold decision, he chose science as his stream. It was a difficult path, one that many considered to be demanding and stressful. His friends were surprised by his choice, especially given his usual laid-back attitude towards life.

Many of Viyaan's peers found it hard to believe that he was serious about his decision. They thought that with his carefree approach, he wouldn't take such a challenging stream seriously. After all, they had always seen him as someone who preferred to enjoy life and take things as they came.

Viyaan, however, was not one to back away from a challenge. He calmly told his friends that he had prepared thoroughly for the exams, but they weren't convinced. They couldn't help but wonder if he had truly changed, or if his carefree attitude was still present, even with such an important milestone ahead of him.

The day the results were released, there was a buzz of excitement and anxiety in the air. Viyaan's friends, who had doubted him, couldn't believe their eyes when they saw his grades. He had done exceptionally well. It was a triumph not just for him, but for everyone who had underestimated his abilities.

The grades confirmed something everyone had suspected but never said aloud, Viyaan was capable of much more than he let on. The sense of accomplishment was undeniable, and while he didn't gloat, he knew he had achieved something significant.

But school was nearing its end. The final year was fast approaching, and Viyaan found himself thinking about what the future held.

Though he had many friends at school, his focus seemed to shift. He started considering relationships again, but he was wary of dating anyone from his immediate circle. The last three girls he had dated had all been from the same group of friends, and in each case, the relationships had ended in disappointment.

The pattern was clear: after two months, things would fizzle out. Viyaan wasn't sure what went wrong, but he began to question whether he should date anyone from his group at all.

He knew that his options were still plentiful, as girls admired his charisma and easygoing nature. However, he was hesitant to dive into another relationship, especially given his past experiences.

Viyaan didn't want to make the same mistakes again, nor did he want to risk complicating things further with his friends. He began to entertain the idea of meeting someone outside of his circle, someone who didn't have any preconceived notions of who he was or what he had been through.

One evening, there was a party at his society's clubhouse, and Viyaan, along with all his friends, was in attendance. The atmosphere was electric, filled with music and laughter as everyone mingled and danced.

Viyaan wasn't particularly interested in staying in one place for too long, but he found himself wandering towards the corner of the room, where a familiar face stood. It was Aadiya, someone he had known for a while but never really gotten to know deeply. She was a year younger than him, yet they had always shared a casual friendship.

Viyaan had always respected Aadiya, but tonight something felt different. Perhaps it was the way the soft glow of the party lights highlighted her features or the way her laughter blended seamlessly with the music, but he felt drawn to her. He made his way over, flashing his usual confident smile, and greeted her casually. Aadiya was surprised to see him approaching, but she welcomed his company, and the two of them began to chat.

As they spoke, Viyaan found himself intrigued by her calm demeanor. Aadiya didn't seem impressed by his usual charm, nor did she fall into the trap of complimenting him like others often did. She had a genuine interest in the conversation, which was refreshing. For once, Viyaan didn't feel like he had to perform or impress anyone. It was just the two of them, talking as equals.

He noticed, however, that the old patterns were beginning to surface again, the familiar feeling of the player in him wanting to start the chase. Viyaan wasn't sure if this was another momentary attraction or if something deeper was beginning to take root. Aadiya was different from the others. She had her own set of values and was clearly not just looking for someone to pass the time with. It intrigued him.

The night went on, and Viyaan found himself increasingly caught up in the rhythm of the conversation with Aadiya. It wasn't just about flirting or impressing her anymore. He began to realize that he was genuinely enjoying her company in a way that was different from his past relationships. For the first time in a while, Viyaan was considering something more meaningful, though he still wasn't sure what it would mean for both of them.

As the party drew to a close, Viyaan couldn't help but feel a sense of anticipation. Could this be the beginning of something new? Or was it just another fleeting connection? Only time would tell. But for the first time in a long while, Viyaan wasn't looking for answers right away. He was content to let things unfold naturally, unsure of where it would take him, but intrigued by the possibility of what lay ahead with Aadiya The **PLAYER's PLAY** had started again.

CHAPTER TWO

THE BOLD ERA

Aadiya was a girl from Viyaan's neighborhood. He had always seen her around, but never really thought much about her, until one night at a party. That night changed everything. Viyaan didn't know why, but something about Aadiya caught his attention in a way it never had before.

They had been friends for a while, but tonight felt different. It wasn't just the lights or the music that made the air feel alive. It was Aadiya.

He noticed how her laughter sounded like music, how her smile could light up the entire room. For the first time, he felt drawn to her in a way he didn't understand. Aadiya, too, seemed to feel the same shift.

As the night went on, they found themselves talking more than usual. They started with small talk, like the weather and the party, but as they continued, the conversation turned deeper.

They began talking about their families, their dreams, and what they wanted out of life. Viyaan realized he had never really known Aadiya in this way before. It felt like they were seeing each other for the first time.

They decided to take a short walk outside to get away from the noise of the party. The cool night air felt refreshing, and the stars above seemed brighter than usual. They walked in comfortable silence for a while, but there was an undeniable tension between them.

"I didn't know you thought about things like this," Viyaan said, breaking the silence. "You've always seemed so calm, so... collected."

Aadiya smiled, looking thoughtful. "I guess we all have different sides to us, sides we don't always show right away. Sometimes it takes the right person to bring them out."

They continued walking and talking, and as the night wore on, they grew even closer. Every laugh, every shared memory, every moment of silence between them felt like it was leading to something more.

Viyaan started to realize that he liked Aadiya, not just as a friend, but in a different way, Aadiya, too, seemed to feel the same way. They didn't need words to know that something special was happening between them.

The next time they were alone at a party, things shifted even further. They found a quiet spot away from the crowd, and without saying much, Viyaan leaned in. Aadiya, looking into his eyes, did the same. It was a simple kiss. They had crossed a line, and there was no going back.

From that point on, they spent more time together. They took walks, had late-night talks, and shared moments of laughter and vulnerability. People started noticing the connection between them.

Their friends began asking Viyaan about Aadiya, about what was going on between them. At first, Viyaan didn't know how to answer. But then he realized it was simple: he liked Aadiya.

That moment marked the beginning of something **BOLD**. They weren't just a couple who had found each other by chance. They were two people who had taken a risk, stepped out of their comfort zones, and decided to see where their connection could take them.

Their relationship wasn't perfect. They had their disagreements, their awkward moments, and their challenges. But through it all, they had something real. They had each other.

Their relationship was bold, because it wasn't afraid to be vulnerable, to take chances, and to grow.

"Love can exist in the most poisonous or the purest form."

Everything was moving fast, and neither Aadiya nor Viyaan could deny it. They were spending almost every night together, caught up in their new connection. Both were in their final year of high school, and with graduation around the corner, they couldn't help but wonder where this all would lead.

One night, their social circle hosted a party, one of those typical gatherings where everyone came together to have fun and let loose before the pressure of exams started. Aadiya and Viyaan attended, their hands often finding each other under the table, a simple gesture that spoke volumes about their closeness.

There was a quiet understanding between them, something beyond words. They didn't need to say much to communicate. Just being close to each other felt like enough.

But the night took a turn when someone unexpected walked in. A person from Viyaan's past, a former classmate from his tuition days showed up at the party. This person, a year older than Viyaan, had always seemed to notice Aadiya from afar.

Viyaan could tell that this person's gaze lingered on Aadiya longer than usual, and he wasn't sure how he felt about it. There was an unspoken tension in the air, something subtle but undeniable, as if this newcomer's attention could somehow disrupt what they had.

The reality of their relationship hit Viyaan in that moment. He realized just how much he had come to care for Aadiya. It wasn't just about the moments they shared, it was about the way they made each other feel.

The way their connection had deepened over the past few weeks made everything else seem insignificant, yet now, in the presence of this other person, Viyaan couldn't ignore the protective instinct rising within him. He could see the interest in the other person's eyes, and it stirred something inside him that he hadn't expected.

The night carried on, but Viyaan couldn't shake the feeling that how things were going. Whether it was the way the other person looked at Aadiya, or the thought of something new entering their lives, he wasn't sure. All he knew was that this was the moment where he realized just how important Aadiya had become to him. He wasn't ready to let go of this feeling, not yet.

this jealousy or Possessiveness came out on Viyaans face was because a day before Viyaan handed her a small box. Inside was a delicate chain, its simplicity yet elegance catching the light.

She looked up at him, surprised by the gesture. It wasn't something he had done before, and the look in his eyes told her that this wasn't just a piece of jewelry,it was a symbol. A symbol of how much she meant to him.

But after that night, *The three formed an unspoken triangle.*

" However, a THIRD person can occasionally be equally present in a relationship between two people without either of them realising it"

Though they were still spending time together and having fun, things between Aadiya and Viyaan weren't going well a month after they started dating. What had initially seemed like a perfect relationship began to change.

Instead of enjoying each other's company, they found themselves bickering more often. The arguments started becoming frequent, and neither of them knew how to stop it. What used to be carefree and easy had turned into a constant cycle of frustration.

Viyaan, who had never been fond of conflict, started feeling the weight of the situation. He wasn't used to the constant tension and didn't know how to handle it anymore.

He realized that the relationship, which once felt so right, was becoming unhealthy. The joy and excitement were replaced with unnecessary arguments and stress. After thinking it through, Viyaan decided to take action. He knew it was time to address the situation and make a decision about what was best for both of them.

Viyaan thought to himself, "I don't know, something just feels off about our relationship. After that party, I couldn't stop thinking about how Aadiya spoke with that guy. I really didn't like it at all."

Often, ego is something that ruin things. But Viyaan's ego didn't teach him to be humble. It caused him discomfort, and he thought ending things would be the right solution. *Sometimes, the decisions we make, though driven by ego, feel like the right ones for ourselves. But in reality, fixing a relationship is more important.*

Ego can cloud our judgment, and in the heat of the moment, we may think walking away is the only option. However, it's also crucial to understand that, sometimes, relationships need effort and compromise. *True strength isn't always in being right; sometimes, it's in putting aside our ego and working through the issues.* After all, love and understanding take precedence over pride.

It's easy to let small things escalate when we don't take a step back and reflect. Viyaan knew he was upset, but deep down, he also understood that his relationship with Aadiya was worth more than his bruised ego. He had to decide if he wanted to hold onto his pride or take a step toward fixing what was broken but Viyaan being Viyaan.

He made the tough decision to **END THINGS** with Aadiya. It came as a shock to her because everything had seemed fine just days before. She didn't expect it to end so suddenly. Usually, when relationships end, people are upset, hurt, or cry. But for Viyaan, it was different.

He actually felt relieved. The tension and constant fighting had made everything feel toxic, and he knew he was better off without it. But Aadiya's reaction wasn't what he expected. She didn't fall apart; instead, she quickly moved on, surprising everyone, including Viyaan.

To his shock, Aadiya started dating someone else. It wasn't just anyone, it was that guy from the party, Avirag. He was a good athlete, living in the same society as Aadiya. Aadiya had a few boys interested in her, but she chose Avirag.

Viyaan couldn't help but feel hurt, but at the same time, a part of him felt relieved. The **breakup** had freed him, and now he could focus on other things.

"Mohabbat jab zehar hojaaye toh rishte se zyadda khud ko zakhm milte hai"("When love turns to poison, it is the self that suffers more than the relationship.")

Aadiya's new relationship made waves within their social circle. Viyaan's friends were surprised, especially because of how quickly she had moved on. But what really bothered Viyaan was the fact that Aadiya had chosen Avirag. He couldn't help but feel a sense of laughter.

He had never imagined Aadiya would choose him, of all people, and yet she did. The memory of the party and how everything had fallen apart kept running through his mind.

But for the next few months, Viyaan focused on his studies and tried to forget about everything that had happened. His life was much more relaxed now, with fewer worries.

The constant tension between him and Aadiya was gone, and he felt like he could finally breathe again. His marks started improving, the past seven months had been a journey of self-improvement in terms of academics.

But life wasn't all about academics. One day, **again** a cricket match between their societies was arranged. Viyaan's team won the toss and chose to bowl first.

It was a crucial match, and both teams were determined to win. Viyaan's team got off to a strong start, taking four wickets early. The opposition was only able to score 78 runs in the first 10 overs, which seemed like a manageable target.

However, as the game went on, things started to shift. The opposition's players began hitting boundaries, and the game became more intense. After 15 overs, their score had risen to 134-5, and Viyaan's team began to lose their composure.

Despite the pressure, Viyaan and his team didn't give up. They put their best bowlers on the field, and the final five overs were crucial. The opposition scored another 20 runs, bringing their total to 154-6 by the end of their innings. Viyaan's team was a little tense.

They knew they could have stopped the opposition from scoring more, but the score was still chaseable. They had confidence in their batting, but they also knew it wouldn't be easy.

The match began with Viyaan's team opening the batting. The first five overs were great; they scored 46-0, thanks to one of the best players, who immediately took charge and hit several boundaries. The team felt confident, but then, two quick wickets fell. Viyaan, though, wasn't going to give up.

He and the other batsman started hitting the bowlers hard, and after 10 overs, the score was 112-2. Viyaan had scored an impressive 41 runs off 19 balls, his best innings so far.

At that point, one of the best players on Viyaan's team had made 51 runs off 31 balls. But then, the match took another turn. Viyaan was out, leaving the team a bit shaken. However, Manit, a versatile all-rounder, stepped up.

He kept the score ticking over with singles, while the team's best player kept smashing boundaries. But after hitting a fantastic 65 runs off 37 balls, the best player was out. Now, it was up to Manit to finish the game. With a calm mind, he hit a four that sealed the win for Viyaan's team.

The game was a complete victory for them. Viyaan's team celebrated their hard-earned win. It had been a tough match, and at one point, it seemed like they might not pull through.

But with solid teamwork, determination, and a bit of luck, they managed to chase down the target and win. The celebration wasn't just about winning; it was about proving themselves that they could work together under pressure and come out on top.

"Aur sabse khubsurat uski yeh aakhie thi..."("And the most beautiful thing was her eyes...**_)_**

There was something happening between Viyaan and a girl named Viyaara. During the game, they exchanged constant eye contact as their friends gathered to watch. The saying, *"eyes are the most beautiful way of communicating,"* truly applied in that moment. But other than that, nothing else seemed to make sense. The connection between them felt different, but no one could figure out what it meant.

Viyaan felt different that day. His heart raced in a way he couldn't explain, and there was a strange, unsettling feeling that something was about to happen.

It wasn't fear, but more like an anticipation that tugged at him. He tried to focus on his usual routine, but his mind kept wandering, unsure about the emotions swirling inside him.

Was it anxiety or excitement? He couldn't decide, but he knew something was shifting within him. He needed time to understand what he was truly feeling, but it was hard to ignore.

In the midst of this confusion, Viyaara crossed his path, and everything seemed to pause for a moment. She had a way of drawing his attention, effortlessly making him think about things he had never considered before.

There was something about her presence, her energy, that left him questioning the possibility of them being more than just two people who occasionally crossed each other's lives.

Every glance and every small conversation felt meaningful, as though there was an unspoken connection between them, yet Viyaan wasn't sure if he was just imagining things.

Could there be a possibility of them becoming closer? Viyaan found himself asking this over and over, though he didn't have an answer. He had always kept his distance, afraid of what might happen if he let his guard down.

But with Viyaara, everything felt different. Maybe it was the way she looked at him, or maybe it was the way her words lingered in his mind long after their conversations ended.

Still, as much as he wanted to believe in the possibility, he wasn't ready to dive in just yet. He was still figuring out what this feeling really was, and whether it was something worth exploring.

"Na jaane kya hua tha, thi voh hamesha se mere pass lekin uss din ke baad se voh hone laggi thi mere dil ke pass"("Not sure what had happened, she was always by my side, but after that day, she started to be close to my heart.")

After around 4-5 days following the match, their friends began to notice the subtle closeness between Viyaan and Viyaara. It wasn't anything overt, just small moments here and there that gave the impression something had shifted between them.

Whether it was the way they looked at each other or the conversations they shared, the signs were becoming hard to ignore.

Soon, as curiosity grew among their group of friends, the topic of Viyaan and Viyaara began circulating. The questions were inevitable. "Are they together?" "What's going on between them?" The chatter grew louder, and before long, it became clear, Viyaan and Viyaara were officially dating.

Very fast right? but that's what makes the story of Viyaan and Viyaara different from others.

What led to this? What had happened in those few days that shifted their relationship from simple friends to something more? The answers weren't immediately clear to anyone, not even to Viyaan and Viyaara themselves. There was no dramatic turning point or clear conversation that defined the change.

It just... happened. Something had sparked between them, and before they knew it, they found themselves in a new, uncharted territory.

What would this new chapter bring? Would it last, or was it just another fleeting moment? Viyaan couldn't help but wonder about the future.

With Viyaan and Viyaara now officially together, the questions didn't stop there. Everyone around them was eager to know more, to understand what was really happening behind the scenes.

But even Viyaan couldn't offer clear answers. He wasn't sure what to expect or how things would play out. There was still a lingering fear in the back of his mind, a fear of repeating the mistakes of the past, of experiencing heartbreak once more.

Would this lead to another painful breakup? Would the trust they were building falter, like so many others before? The uncertainty was overwhelming at times. Viyaan couldn't ignore the voice in his head questioning the authenticity of what was unfolding.

And yet, despite all the doubt and uncertainty, something felt different this time. There was a warmth in the way Viyaara looked at him, a certain comfort in their conversations, that Viyaan couldn't ignore. Perhaps this was the beginning of something real, something worth exploring further. But the future remained uncertain, and Viyaan wasn't ready to make any **bold** declarations just yet.

He found himself torn between hope and caution, unsure whether he should fully invest in this relationship or guard his heart just a little longer. The emotions swirling inside him were complex, and for the first time in a while, he wasn't sure what path to take.

Two years passed since that moment of change. A lot had happened in the interim, and life had continued to move forward for both Viyaan and Viyaara. Their relationship, though filled with ups and downs, had survived and grown. But change was inevitable, and it always came when least expected.

Something was about to happen, something that would shift the course of their lives once again. What that change would be, and why it was about to occur, was a mystery that loomed over them.

The story wasn't over, and what lay ahead remained unknown. But Viyaan knew one thing for certain the path ahead would change them both, and it was a journey he couldn't yet predict.

As time passed, Viyaan found himself reflecting on everything that had led to this point. From the first spark between him and Viyaara to the moments of doubt and the bond they had built, it all felt like a whirlwind. He had grown, changed, and learned so much about himself and the people around him.

Viyaan wasn't sure what would happen next, but he was ready to face it with Viyaara by his side. What would the next chapter bring? Only time would tell. The story, after all, was far from over.

Despite the uncertainty, there was an undeniable pull that kept them together. Viyaan and Viyaara's connection had deepened over time.

What had started as a quiet bond had transformed into something more meaningful. They had shared moments of vulnerability, supported each other during challenging times, and built something that felt worth fighting for.

Life had a way of surprising him, and he knew better than to assume he had everything figured out.

For now, though, Viyaan was content to enjoy the present. He and Viyaara had come a long way together. Their journey had been anything but predictable, yet it had been real. As they both moved forward into the unknown, they were learning how to navigate life's twists and turns together.

What the future held was uncertain, but for the first time in a long time, Viyaan wasn't afraid of it. With Viyaara by his side, whatever came next felt like something they could face together. **The story was far from over, and they were just getting started.**

CHAPTER THREE

THE PLAYER GOT PLAYED

Viyaan had never experienced feelings for a girl like this before. It was something completely new to him. As the saying goes, **once you fall in love, you can't stop feeling how it changes you.** Love has a way of opening your heart in unexpected ways, and that's exactly what happened to Viyaan.

Everything around him seemed brighter, and every little moment with her felt special. His feelings for her grew stronger with each passing day. He couldn't stop thinking about her, wondering how she was feeling and if she felt the same way. But one thing was certain he felt a different rush with Viyaara that even he dosent know.

Viyaara, on the other hand, was so in love that she didnt know how to approach this feeling. She didn't want to feel things quickly, but she knew that Viyaan had been there for her in ways that others hadn't. She appreciated everything he did for her."Viyaan is my first boyfriend, I dont know I love him the way I feel it it movies and I may be drawn to him too much" said Viyaara to her friends. "I dont trust this guy he has always been a player and never respected the feelings of others" replied her friends.

Her friends, gave her a variety of suggestions. Some of them thought she should be more open with Viyaan, to be clear about her feelings, while others recommended she take her time and see where things naturally went. Viyaara was confused.

Every suggestion seemed to contradict the other, and she felt overwhelmed. What was the right thing to do? How could she make a decision when she wasn't sure about her own emotions? Despite their advice, Viyaara still had no idea what the right choice was, and she was left feeling uncertain and unsure about how to move forward.

Time passed, and a whole month went by without much happening between the two of them. Viyaan continued to care deeply for Viyaara, but he couldn't ignore the growing distance between them. There were fewer conversations, fewer shared moments, and less time spent together.

Viyaan started to question if Viyaara even cared about him as much as he cared about her. The connection he had felt before seemed to fade away. It was as if they were two different people on two separate paths, moving further apart with each passing day.

He tried not to think too much about it, but the doubt crept into his mind. He wondered if perhaps their relationship was having only one-sided efforts. He had always been the one to reach out, to make the effort to spend time with her.

But now, she was spending more and more time with her other friends, and Viyaan was left feeling ignored. Every time he saw her laughing with her friends or chatting with them, he couldn't help but feel extreme jealousy. Was she losing interest in him? Was this the end of whatever bond they had shared?

As the days went on, Viyaan's feelings of uncertainty grew stronger. He began to believe that maybe there was no future for them. Perhaps they were better off as friends, or perhaps there was just no connection between them anymore.

It hurt him to think that way, but the distance and silence were becoming too loud to ignore. He started to think that it might be better to end things now, before it hurt even more later. He told himself that it was the right thing to do, even though it felt painful.

"Apne waqt mai ishq ki kadar karlo verna vahi ishq tumhare haath se waqt ko lejaayega"("Value love in your time, or else that very love will take time away from you.")

The two-month anniversary of their meeting was just around the corner, and Viyaara had finally made a decision. After much thought and reflection, she had picked out a gift for Viyaan. She wanted it to be special, a token of appreciation for all the kindness he had shown her.

It wasn't just a gift; it was a way of telling him that she valued him. She had been unsure for so long, but now, she felt ready to express all her feelings through this gesture. She hoped it would mean something to him.

The day before their anniversary, Viyaan called her. His voice sounded distant, and there was a certain finality in his words. He told her that he didn't feel the connection anymore, that he thought it was best for both of them to move on.

He said that their relationship wasn't going anywhere, and he didn't want to keep pretending. Viyaan's heart felt heavy as he spoke, but it was clear to him that it was time to let go. He didn't want to drag things out, and he thought that calling it quits now would be the best decision.

Viyaara was stunned. She hadn't expected this at all. Her heart sank, and she could feel the tears welling up in her eyes. How had things gotten to this point? She had been so unsure about her feelings, but she had never wanted to hurt Viyaan.

The gift she had bought for him now felt meaningless, and the idea of seeing him face to face seemed impossible. She had never imagined that things would end like this, especially after everything they had been through together.

Viyaara started crying, overwhelmed by the shock of what had just happened. She couldn't understand how everything had unraveled so quickly. It was as if the world had turned upside down in an instant. "I...I.. What did I do? I hate him, how could he do this just a day before!" said Viayara. She felt betrayed by her own emotions, unsure whether she had been too slow to realize what she felt or if she had just been too distant.

Her friends quickly gathered around her, rushing to offer comfort and support. They hugged her, told her everything would be okay, and reassured her that it wasn't her fault. But no words could truly ease the pain. Everyone seemed so concerned, but Viyaara couldn't stop crying. The tears flowed uncontrollably, and she felt completely lost. How had this all happened? Was it something she could have prevented?

Some of her friends stayed longer, asking her what had happened. They wanted to know the details, to help her make sense of the situation, but Viyaara didn't have the answers. She couldn't explain why things had ended so suddenly, and she certainly couldn't explain why she had felt the way she had. It was all so confusing, and the pain was still fresh in her heart.

Viyaara knew that this chapter of her life had come to a close BUT WAS IT REALLY CLOSED? remember what I said *"Ishq tumhare haath se waqt ko lejaayega"*(love will take time away from you) it will unfold later on , but she wasn't sure where the next one would lead.

All she could do was take it one step at a time, knowing that eventually, the pain would lessen. But for now, she could only cry, surrounded by the people who cared about her, and hope that someday, she would understand what had happened between her and Viyaan.

Viyaan claimed that he was astounded by the turn of events. He couldn't believe that Viyaara was giving him less of her time. For a while, it had seemed like everything was fine between them, but now, it felt like there was a growing distance.

Viyaan had always been the one to put effort into their connection, but lately, it felt like he was the only one trying. He had given so much of himself to her, and now, the sudden lack of attention from her left him feeling confused and hurt. How could things have changed so quickly?.

Viyaara hadn't expected this to happen, but as things went on, she realized that sometimes, no one can predict the future. Life has a way of changing things without warning, and sometimes the feelings we think we can control become unpredictable.

For a while, Viyaan was left to wonder whether there was any chance for things to improve. He had no answers, no clear way forward. His thoughts were a whirlwind of confusion and frustration. He was hurt by the distance that had grown between them, but he also knew that he couldn't force someone to feel something they didn't.

The uncertainty weighed heavily on him, and he needed time to process everything. He told himself he would focus on his upcoming college entrance exams, believing that they would give him some time away from the situation to think things through.

As the college entrance exams approached, Viyaan tried to focus on his studies, but he was UNAWARE that a sting of HEARTBREAK was in store for him.

We cannot predict life and certainly we cannot predict a word called "Karma" it often comes back to you when you are needed to remind that you never had been kind to other people when they were kind to you. Viyaan put all his focus on studies and came with the peace that he'll enjoy his college life.

And then, just as he thought things might begin to settle, life threw something unexpected at him, COVID-19. The pandemic shocked everyone in India, throwing the world into a state of uncertainty. Schools and colleges closed, social life came to a standstill, and everything that had once felt so familiar suddenly became unfamiliar.

Life seemed to pause, and people had to adjust to a new reality. The restrictions were everywhere, and even though there were some relaxations allowed, it was clear that the world would never be the same again.

In the midst of all this, Viyaan found himself in an even more complicated situation. He had tried to focus on his studies, but now, there was even more free time than he knew what to do with. He wasn't able to distract himself as much anymore, and with that came a lot of time for reflection.

His thoughts turned inward, and he began to reevaluate his feelings and what he wanted out of life. It was during this time that he realized he had been missing something important: *connection*.

"Connection is a word that if in mobile phones, systems and in real life forms, everything runs smooth but when it breaks...*YOU* break"

During the pandemic, Viyaan reconnected with someone from his past, a girl he had known for seven years. They had been friends for a long time, and their bond has never been a strong one, built only on years of familiarity.

As the months went by, something began to shift between them. Viyaan had always cared for her in a way, but he had never seriously considered anything more than friendship. However, as time passed, he began to feel something different.

It wasn't that Viyaan had completely forgotten about Viyaara, but as the days turned into weeks, his feelings for this girl from his past started to grow. He found himself thinking about her more and more.

There was something about their friendship that felt comfortable, something that had always been there beneath the surface. They had both changed over the years, and now, in the midst of this pandemic, Viyaan found himself wondering if maybe they could be more than just friends.

As they spent more time together, talking about life, sharing their thoughts, and supporting each other through the challenges of the lockdown, Viyaan began to realize that his feelings for her were deepening.

He started to see her in a new light, and for the first time in a long while, he felt like he was experiencing a spark of hope again. The connection he had with her felt genuine, and he could see the possibility of something more. It was like a door had opened for him, and he was ready to walk through it.

Viyaan found himself feeling a sense of excitement that he hadn't felt in a long time. He would think about her constantly, looking forward to their next conversation or the next time they would meet, even if it was just virtually.

His heart began to open in ways he hadn't expected, and he found himself considering the future with her. For the first time in a while, he felt like things were falling into place again. Maybe this was the new beginning he needed after everything with Viyaara.

but in this world, the only four-letter word that can make you happy and unhappy at the same time is *"LOVE".*

"What's happening to me? Am I really that attracted to her? I always say, 'Can this be it? My final and long-lasting relationship?'" said Viyaan to himself. Restrictions had just been lifted, and Viyaan firstly arranged a meeting with the girl. Oh right! The girl's name is Chaitrika.

She is from Viyaan's school and has been crushing on him since school, but Viyaan never paid attention. But now time has taken a turn, and Viyaan is madly looking forward to the meetup. Chaitrika is doing MBBS, and she is a very silent girl, opposite to Viyaan. But as the day goes, opposites tend to attract you more.

Finally, they got to meet, and Viyaan just couldn't take his eyes off her. They started having conversations and were full on flirting that day. Something very big happened, Viyaan PROPOSED to her. That's the first time he has done that for someone. Obviously, the answer was yes.

Viyaan took Chaitrika to a date at her favorite restaurant in Delhi, and that was the first time actually Viyaan had put the effort first and went on the date. He had bought her a bracelet indicating how he felt for her, without any warning.

Chaitrika also liked him, but there was a sense of hesitation, not because of Viyaan's reputation, but because she never went to him at first. Viyaan somehow never noticed this, but he was enjoying all his time with her.

None of his friends knew how Viyaan's life was going to change after the day they completed 1 month of dating.

Viyaan started to believe this would last for life because he was genuinely in love with her, but in life..

"There is a concept known as *karma*, and when it arrives, it will **SCARE** you."

The girl on the next day called up Viyaan saying "I dont have feelings for you, Lets part ways!"

Viyaan's entire life seemed to flash before his eyes in an instant. The faces of every woman he had broken up with were suddenly in front of him.

He saw the heartbreak he had caused, the moments when he had walked away without a second thought, leaving them confused and hurt. He hadn't realized it before, but now, as everything came rushing back to him, he saw the damage he had done.

The carefree attitude he had carried with him, the belief that it was always just about having fun and moving on to the next chapter, suddenly felt so hollow. Each relationship, each breakup, had been part of a pattern, and now he couldn't escape the consequences of his actions. It was as though he was being forced to confront the past he had avoided for so long.

A **YEAR** had passed since that realization, and during that time, Viyaan had tried to move on with his life. He threw himself into his college life, focusing on his studies, making new friends, and experiencing the freedom that came with adulthood.

He went on trips, partied with his new friends, and lived the kind of life that many young people do when they're away from home, exploring their independence. He was living in the moment, and for the most part, he felt that there was nothing to regret

He wasn't looking back; he wasn't dwelling on the past. Yet, in the quiet moments, when the excitement of his busy college life faded, the truth kept coming back in.

Viyaan couldn't ignore the feeling that something was missing. Despite all the fun, all the distractions, there was an emptiness inside him.

He had been so focused on moving forward that he hadn't given himself the time to reflect on the people he had hurt, including the women he had left behind without explanation or closure. Over time, that emptiness grew into something more, a deep sense of sadness.

He began to think about the girls he had been with, the ones he had hurt along the way, and he couldn't shake the feeling that maybe, just maybe, he owed them all an apology. He had been so selfish, so caught up in his own desires, that he hadn't thought about how his actions affected them. And now, in this moment of reflection, he realized just how wrong he had been.

He wondered if he could somehow make amends, if there was a way to undo the damage he had caused. He thought about the heartache, the tears, the misunderstandings, and he wondered if they would ever forgive him. But there was something even more surprising, something that shook him to his core.

He had always believed that he was in control, that nothing could catch him off guard, that he could walk away from any relationship without feeling regret. But now, he was feeling something he had never anticipated: the sting of rejection. The shock of someone else leaving him.

At first, he thought he could brush it off. After all, he had always been the one doing the breaking up, and he had always found a way to move on. But this time, it felt different. The shock of Chaitrika ending things with him left him confused.

How could this happen? How could someone else be the one to make that decision? Viyaan had never been in that position before, and it made him realize just how much he had taken everything for granted.

For the first time, he understood what it felt like to be on the receiving end of heartbreak. And, more importantly, he realized how much he had hurt others without truly understanding their feelings.

But now, he was ready to change. He was ready to face his past, no matter how difficult it might be, and take the first step toward making amends. And maybe, just maybe, by doing so, he could find peace within himself. The time for regrets was over, but the time for growth had just begun.

You simply have to deal with the **toughness** that life will present you with as you advance in your career. Life's experiences with love are unique, but they can be overcome. Sometimes, things may not go as you expect, and relationships may not turn out the way you hoped, but those experiences, no matter how difficult they were, shape you.

In every heartbreak or disappointment, there is something to learn, something to grow from. You don't just have to face the challenges; you have to embrace them. You face the pain, the doubts, and the uncertainty, but in doing so, you find strength.

Viyaan transformed completely, becoming more patient, peaceful, and realistic. He understood that life doesn't always go the way you plan, and that sometimes you have to adjust your expectations and accept things as they come.

He was no longer the impulsive person he used to be. He had learned to take things slow, to reflect on his actions, and to be considerate of others' feelings. The lessons he had learned from his past mistakes had shaped him into a better person. He wasn't perfect, but he was striving to be better every day.

He let go of all the negative memories from his former relationships and moved on, becoming a better version of himself. Those memories, once painful, no longer had a hold on him. He had learned to forgive himself, to accept his past, and to make peace with it.

It wasn't easy, but with time, he realized that holding onto bitterness and regret would only weigh him down. So, he let go and focused on becoming the person he wanted to be, a person who could learn from the past but not be defined by it.

Everyone has gone through a phase in their lives where people leave you just when you need them the most. It's one of the most difficult experiences to deal with, especially when you least expect it. For Viyaan, this feeling hit during a period of his life that was already filled with uncertainty and confusion.

But, as difficult as it was, it was also part of his growth, a chapter that would later become a lesson in his life. In his third year of college, Viyaan decided to take a break and traveled to **Goa** with a friend. It was a dream come true for him, a chance to escape the daily grind and enjoy life without the usual stresses.

He had been looking forward to this trip for months, and when the moment finally arrived, he couldn't help but feel a sense of freedom. Viyaan thoroughly enjoyed himself there, surrounded by beautiful beaches, vibrant culture, and a carefree atmosphere.

The weight of the worries and frustrations that had been building up over time seemed to lift from his shoulders. He didn't think of her, the one person who had been on his mind for so long.

The trip offered him a brief but much-needed escape from his emotions, a way to temporarily leave behind the pain he had been carrying. For the first time in a while, he was truly able to enjoy the moment, to live without the lingering thoughts of past heartbreaks.

But moving on from someone is never as simple as just escaping your environment. There are several little challenges you must overcome in order to truly move on from someone. These obstacles aren't physical; they're emotional and mental.

They're the tiny battles you fight within yourself every day. The first challenge is forgetting about them, a process that seems impossible at times. It's not just about putting them out of your mind, it's about completely letting go of the attachment and memories you shared.

The second challenge is resisting the urge to contact them, whether it's through a phone call or a text message. It can be incredibly hard to not reach out, especially when you feel like you want to explain yourself, ask questions, or just hear their voice.

But you have to fight that urge to hold on to something that has already ended. And most importantly, the hardest part is not wanting to discuss what they did to you. The pain of betrayal, disappointment, or sadness can cloud your judgment, and the temptation to talk about it to others or even to the person involved can feel overwhelming.

All of these obstacles were things Viyaan had to face, but over time, he started to realize that the trip to Goa had been more than just a getaway. It had been a turning point for him. When he returned from his trip, everyone saw the changes in him. He was different.

There was a newfound peace in his demeanor, a sense of calm that hadn't been there before. His friends noticed that he seemed more at ease, more relaxed, and even more confident in himself. They were thrilled for him because they could see how much this trip had impacted him.

Viyaan was no longer the person he was before the trip. He had grown. He had started to let go of his past, to stop carrying the weight of old wounds. The trip had given him the perspective he needed to truly move forward.

A realization can come when you least expect it. Viyaan began to understand that while one person can change you and bring out the best in you, it almost always comes at the cost of heartbreak.

The heartbreak is the price you pay for the lessons, the strength, and the growth that come from it. But it's a lesson that not everyone is ready for, and it's one that Viyaan had to learn the hard way.

He now understood that life would present challenges, and love would be no different. You might fall in love, and you might face pain, but each experience would add something valuable to your life.

Viyaan's personal growth didn't come without its own struggles. He had experienced heartbreak on more than one occasion, but this time, it felt different.

In a matter of months, he had broken up with two girls he had been deeply attached to(Viyaara and chaitrika) though he broke up wth viyaara but he was attached to her deeply. He had never experienced such severe heartbreak before, and the emotional toll it took on him was unlike anything he had gone through previously.

Two years had passed since then, and the next year would mark the end of his college career. Looking back, it felt surreal how quickly time had flown. His relationships and connections with his school and society friends were still strong. They never left him and would never leave him.

These friendships had been a constant support, a solid foundation, and he knew they would endure long after college life was over. Through all the ups and downs, his friends had remained by his side, and that bond was something he cherished deeply.

Viyaan was learning a lot for himself, and in turn, he was teaching a lot to others. Over the years, he had grown in many ways, not just in terms of knowledge, but also in personal development. College had opened his eyes to lessons he never expected to learn. It was more than just academics; it was about becoming a better version of himself.

He had become more self-aware, more patient, and more willing to help those around him. It wasn't just about what he could achieve on his own; it was about sharing what he had learned with others. Whether it was giving advice, lending an ear, or offering support, Viyaan realized that these little acts of kindness were just as valuable as the lessons themselves.

Viyaan noticed that the changes within him didn't go unnoticed. His friends, professors, and even he himself acknowledged how much he had grown. These positive efforts were always recognized, which made him feel proud of the progress he had made.

He had come a long way from the person he once was, and the transformation had made him more confident in himself.

He had learned to be a better listener, a more compassionate friend, and someone who was always ready to help. This growth, in every way, made Viyaan feel fulfilled. It was not just about the grades or achievements anymore, it was about the person he was becoming.

However, Viyaan had lost touch with art and craft, areas he had once been deeply passionate about. As life had moved forward, his focus had shifted.

The demands of academics, sports, and personal growth had taken priority, and his creative side had been pushed aside. Though he had always loved working with his hands and exploring new creative ideas, these things no longer seemed to fit into his busy schedule.

Despite the shift, Viyaan was still excelling in the things he had always been good at. His performance in sports and academics remained strong, and he continued to push himself in these areas.

College had its own way of encouraging discovery, but it also required focus and balance. He knew that some things had to be put on the backburner for now.

College life, however, had a unique way of changing things. It wasn't long before Viyaan found himself embracing new experiences. He began attending cricket matches, joining friends for celebrations, and participating in various events that brought people together. The atmosphere at these events was filled with energy, and Viyaan couldn't help but feel the excitement.

The laughter, the competition, and the fun moments with friends reminded him of the joys of living in the present.

These were the moments when he truly felt alive, when he could forget about everything else and simply enjoy the company of those around him.

It wasn't just about the games or the competitions, it was the energy, the friendship, and the memories that came with them.

It was about being present, making memories, and connecting with people. These moments reminded him that life wasn't only about achievements or goals, it was also about having fun and enjoying the time you had.

He understood now that balance was the key. While academics and personal growth were important, so was enjoying the present and building meaningful connections with others. College was teaching him to appreciate life in all its aspects, and for that, Viyaan was grateful and now

he has officialy become "***MAKHMALI(SOFT)***".

CHAPTER FOUR

AGAIN AND ALWAYS

"Jis mohabbat ko peeche chodh kahi duur chala aaya...ae mohabbat tu bhi mere saath bohot duur aake he kyun takraaya?"("The love I left behind and traveled far away... Oh love, why did you come so far and collide with me?")

Viyaan was always wondering how he had survived these **four years** and how he had changed so much from the person he had once been. It felt like a lifetime ago when he first made the decision to leave everything behind and move to **London**.

The transition had been challenging at first, but now, looking back, he realized just how far he had come. In these **four years**, he had learned so many things about life, himself, and the world around him.

His mind often wandered as he thought about his journey, how he had evolved from a carefree college student to someone who now valued discipline, responsibility, and maturity.

Yes, it had been four years since Viyaan left everyone behind and moved to London for further studies. When he first arrived in this new city, he had no idea what to expect.

The city was big, fast, and full of opportunities, but it also felt isolating at times.

He had left behind his friends, his family, and everything familiar to him. It wasn't easy, but the decision to move had been necessary. It was his chance to grow and create a new life. Little did he know, London would become his permanent home, shaping him into the person he was now.

His life was not always the same as it had been in the previous four years. When he first arrived in London, everything felt like an uphill battle. He had been unsure of himself and had faced a lot of loneliness, but with time, he found his place.

He had grown up, stopped playing with people's hearts, and started valuing the relationships he built around him. Viyaan was no longer the impulsive person he used to be, always seeking thrills or attention. He had learned that real happiness came from within, and the importance of emotional connections, trust, and honesty. He began to value these qualities in the people he interacted with.

By now, Viyaan had settled into his new life in London. He was no longer the carefree young man who once made spontaneous decisions based on emotions. Now, he was more grounded, more thoughtful, and more intentional with his actions.

His priorities had changed, and it was evident in the way he approached both his personal and professional life. He had stopped playing games with people's feelings, recognizing the importance of kindness and respect. The mistakes from his past were no longer a part of who he was.

As time passed, Viyaan's confidence grew. He found a circle of friends who shared similar values, and through them, he began to understand the importance of loyalty and support. He had always believed that friendships were about fun and excitement, but now he saw them as lasting bonds that were built on trust and mutual respect.

London, once a place that made him feel small and alone, had become a place where he thrived. The city had shaped him in ways he never imagined, challenging him to grow beyond his comfort zone. Every new experience was a step forward in his personal evolution.

Viyaan had found a balance between his work and his personal life, something he hadn't known how to do when he first arrived. The long hours of studying had paid off, and he had earned the respect of his professors and peers alike.

His hard work was finally beginning to show in his grades and in the opportunities that were opening up for him. What had seemed impossible when he first moved to London now felt like a natural part of his life.

His past mistakes had taught him valuable lessons, and he was ready to face whatever came next with a sense of purpose.

He no longer feared the unknown as he once had. With each day, he felt more confident in his ability to handle the challenges that life threw his way.

Viyaan was now working in an IT firm, where he had secured a stable job after completing his studies. The world of technology was fast-paced and challenging, but it had become a part of his identity. He was learning and growing every day, taking on new projects and responsibilities.

It was a sharp contrast to the young man who had once been so uncertain about his future. Now, he was focused and driven, eager to build a career for himself. He had found purpose in his work, and that gave him a sense of fulfillment that he had never experienced before.

One day, when Viyaan was leaving for a meeting, his boss informed him that a visitor was on the way and wanted to speak with him. Viyaan was a little puzzled. He didn't expect any visitors and couldn't think of anyone who might be coming to see him.

He figured it was likely just another business-related matter. However, as he continued his preparations for the meeting, his curiosity grew. Who could this visitor be? Was it someone from his past? Maybe someone from India who had come to London? The possibilities were endless, and he couldn't shake the feeling that this visit might be more significant than he realized.

He had no idea that this unexpected visitor would bring a sense of nostalgia, and perhaps even stir up old memories from his past. The visitor's arrival would prove to be a turning point, reminding Viyaan of how much had changed in the years since he left India.

You don't want that person to approach you after everything between you went wrong, but that's life. You'll eventually run into them, and you need to be prepared for what you'll need to do.

"Hi! I'm here to meet Viyaan." said the familier voice. Time stopped, viyaan went running to the reception as he might know who the person was. he saw....

"Uss waqt ko mere pass laut ke aate hue dekh raha tha jiski kabhi maine kadar nahi ki..."("I was watching the time returning to me, the one I had never valued before...")

He saw none other than Viyaara...He was startled to see her, and a flood of memories suddenly appeared in front of him. It was as though time had never passed, and everything from the past rushed back in an instant. But because he had changed, he didn't shy away.

Instead, he took the initiative to apologise, something he would not have done before. He was no longer the same person he once was. This change in him had been a long journey, one that involved self-reflection and growth.

Viyaara was taken aback by his apology. She hadn't expected this. But as they stood there, it was clear that something had shifted between them. Slowly, they began to chat, just like they had when they were friends. The conversation was easy, as if nothing had ever happened between them.

They spoke freely, with the comfort of old friends rekindling their connection. Neither of them brought up the past, perhaps because they both realized that it no longer mattered. What was important was the present moment, and the fact that they were talking again, after all this time.

For both of them, there was a sense of familiarity and comfort in their renewed friendship. Days turned into weeks, and weeks into months. They started talking every day and began meeting up regularly. It was as though they had picked up where they left off, as if no time had passed. Their bond was rediscovered, and it seemed as though nothing had changed between them.

But the truth was, things had changed. Both Viyaan and Viyaara had grown. They had experienced their own personal journeys, and now they were different people.

However, there was a restored faith in each other, a trust that had been lost but now seemed to return, stronger than before. Viyaan was different with her, and he knew it. He had never behaved this way with anyone in the **four years** that had passed.

It was as though their past friendship had never truly left him. The old comfort and trust were still there, waiting to be rekindled.

The best thing to do is move on, and Viyaara had already done so. She had accepted the changes in both of their lives and had made peace with the past. She wasn't holding onto old wounds, and she was ready to move forward.

She had grown as well, and was no longer the person she once was when they had first known each other. But this didn't mean that their friendship couldn't be revived. It was simply a new chapter, one that both of them were ready to begin.

But the question was, why was Viyaan discovering a soft corner for Viyaara? Sometimes, we don't realize when we develop feelings for someone, especially when we aren't even looking for it.

Viyaan had always felt something for Viyaara, something more than anyone else, and reuniting with her after four years made him feel different.

He had spent so much time being alone, shutting himself off from relationships, yet now, he was finding himself building something real with her, without any second thoughts, even with the person he had once broken the bond with.

This was a big change for him, as he had long stopped believing in relationships after his past experiences. He had distanced himself from emotional connections, not trusting that they could last. But with Viyaara, things felt different.

The bond they had shared years ago seemed to have resurfaced, and Viyaan found himself wanting to nurture it this time. He no longer felt the fear or hesitation that once held him back; he was allowing himself to experience something real, even though it was with someone he had once walked away from.

However, this came with a price. Viyaan wasn't ready for the emotions that were beginning to stir inside him. He hadn't expected to feel this vulnerable again, and he wasn't sure how to handle the intensity of what was growing between him and Viyaara.

It scared him, but at the same time, it intrigued him. He knew that opening himself up meant risking pain, but for the first time in a long time, he was willing to take that chance.

Then one day, Viyaara told Viyaan about a guy. She casually mentioned him, unaware of the effect it would have on him. There was a brief pause in the conversation. Viyaan's **heart skipped a beat**, and his mind went quiet for a moment. He had known something only **he could understand**. He could feel something in his chest, but he didn't let it show. **His eyes gave away more than he intended**, though.

His smile was **steady**, but his eyes spoke volumes, he was feeling a mix of emotions that no one could possibly imagine. He had kept his feelings hidden, but in that moment, it was clear to him what he truly felt.

The conversation that took place was about viyaara asking for help that is, Viyaara was unsure about what to do. She has now been careful with her feelings and, she was interested in a guy. She wasn't sure how to make him notice her or how to approach the situation. It was a tricky feeling to have.

She had never been in this position before, and it made her feel uncertain. She knew she liked him, but did he feel the same? She thought about all the different ways she could handle this, but nothing seemed clear. She decided to talk to Viyaan.

She trusted him, and she knew that he would give her the advice she needed. She needed to hear from someone who had been through similar things, someone who could help her figure out what steps to take next.

The next day, Viyaan talked to his friend about everything that had happened and what was going on. His friend noticed something unusual, Viyaan, in these four years, had never shared a story with such laughter, sadness, and conviction.

It was as if there was more to the story that Viyaan wasn't saying. His friend, curious, asked, "It's great that you're willing to help her, but why did you pause when you said, 'She's interested in a guy'?"

At that moment, no one had an answer. Viyaan didn't fully understand why he had reacted that way either. But deep down, he knew that time would eventually reveal the answers to the questions they both had. Life had a way of unfolding, and sometimes, it took time to truly understand the reasons behind our actions.

Viyaan said to himself, "What has happened to me? The people I left behind to come this far, now it's hard to live without them. I'm in a foreign land, but I still feel a sense of belonging. I have broken her heart, yet I still want to mend it. Anyway, if anyone is meant to be with her better than I ever could, I will make sure she's happy and send her away with all my blessings."

"You tend to like people the most when you're at your lowest, because in those moments, you need someone to help lift you up."

Viyaan and Viyaara were both strong together once more, but this time fate didn't want them together, and one of them would *ALWAYS* suffer.

Viyaan didn't know the solution, but he knew he had to help Viyaara. He couldn't just stand by without doing anything. He had to be there for her, no matter how complicated things seemed.

After work, Viyaan went to a coffee shop and met the guy. The guy was well-built and seemed fascinating. Viyaan couldn't help but notice how confident and charming he appeared.

Even though the three of them were speaking, it seemed like one more partcipant was trying to add something. Why "participation"? Because of Viyaan's **eyes**, they wanted to say much more than Viyaara could possibly imagine, yet he smiled and remained supportive throughout.

"mohabbat ke roop anek hai lekin sabse khubsurart aur dard dene waala roop jaane dena hai..."("Love has many forms, but the most beautiful and painful form is the one that must be let go...")

He went to speak to the guy because he knew that Viyaara mattered to someone else more than she did to him, even though he valued her more than any other person in his life. Viyaan couldn't ignore the fact that the guy was clearly interested in her.

But at the same time, he felt a deep responsibility toward Viyaara, knowing how much her trust had been shaken over the years.

The guy seemed to like her, but Viyaan noticed the hesitation in his actions. He could tell that the guy was afraid she wouldn't say yes, mainly because she had lost trust in men. Viyaan could see that the uncertainty in the guy's heart mirrored his own.

How do you expect Viyaara to say yes? Because 'Ek **ladki ki mohabbat mai itni taakat hoti hai ki jis din uski voh mohabbat tut jaaye voh kabhi kisi aur ko apni**

mohabbat nhi maanegi.'("A girl's love has so much power that the day her love breaks, she will never accept anyone else's love as her own.") Viyaara had already lost one person she truly loved before, and now she's afraid of opening her heart again.

She couldn't bear the thought of trusting someone so deeply only to get hurt again. At this moment, all she needed was comfort from an old friend, someone who understood her pain.

It's not uncommon for people who have been hurt in love to close themselves off. When you've experienced a deep, emotional loss, it's hard to open up to new possibilities. Viyaara's heart had already been broken once, and the idea of giving her love to someone else felt too risky.

The fear of being hurt again overshadowed any hope of moving forward. But sometimes, in such moments of vulnerability, we find ourselves reaching out to old friends for support. Friends who were once a part of our life and who understood us before all the pain came.

Old friendships often provide comfort in ways that new relationships can't. With a friend who has been there through thick and thin, you don't need to explain yourself. They just know. They understand the weight you carry without having to say a word. And for someone like Viyaara, who was too afraid to trust again, this was all she needed, a familiar voice, a gentle reminder that not all connections lead to heartbreak.

Sometimes, it takes the presence of someone who cares, someone who's known you before the hurt, to help you start healing. Though Viyaara couldn't yet let go of her fear, she found solace in knowing that there were still people around her who would help her through the pain, even if it wasn't in the way she expected.

Viyaan made the decision to confront Viyaara. He realized that **he was, in part, to blame** for her loss of trust. Viyaan warned Viyaara not to act foolishly and not to believe that the guy was like him. He reminded her how beautiful she is in love and how much people are willing to do for her when they are in love with her.

"Hey, you are the most beautiful girl in this world, but I'm not saying this just to flatter you. I could say a lot of nice things about you, but the truth is, you're such a simple and calm person. Your eyes speak a lot, they say so much that even someone who doesn't understand can get it. As for my mistakes, I deserve the punishment myself. I was really foolish. **Words like love are really heavy for me**, and I don't think I can handle them. Even if you don't love me anymore, it's okay. You're not like me, you see the good in people, and that makes you the most beautiful girl in this world. Well, I've said too much now. Haha, you should go to him, talk to him, and say everything you need to."

Viyaara went up to the guy to propose him immediatly, Viyaan was seeing them from outisde and he saw them hugging and his tears started to come out. He was still smiling, though. It wasn't sadness; it was a mix of emotions. He was happy for her, knowing that she had found a better man. Viyaan had always wanted what was best for her, even if that meant **letting her go**.

"To confront people, we say a lot of things, but only our heart knows the real truth. We might hide our emotions, but our eyes never lie."

Viyaan had been through so many different phases in his love life. But this time, something was different. He was proud of himself for **letting go** of the girl he had loved, knowing that she loved someone else so much.

"Mere saath thi toh uski yehi mere liye mohabbat thi aur mujhe nahi, per jab mujhse duur gayi toh voh meri he ibbadat ban gayi" ("When she was with me, her love was for me, and when she went away from me, she became my devotion.")

It had taken him a while to realize, but he understood now that he couldn't give her the love she deserved. He looked at her happiness and felt a sense of peace. It wasn't easy, but he knew it was the right thing to do. He returned to his regular schedule, feeling a little lighter than before. He had let go, and it felt good.

But little did he know, life had a way of changing things again. He had no idea what would come next, and how his life would turn yet again.

It had been a while since Viyaan had seen both of them, so he went to the house, but no one was there. He felt a strange unease as he stood at the door, wondering where they could be. He knocked, but there was no answer.

It was as if they had just vanished without a trace. Later, he learned that both had moved, which shocked him. He had never imagined this. Viyaan had thought that she had left without ever having the chance to meet him. His mind raced as he tried to make sense of it all, wondering why things had ended this way.

He tried to talk to everyone he could, asking if anyone knew where they had gone, but nobody had any answers. No one knew why they had left, or where they had gone. It was frustrating, and Viyaan felt more lost with every passing day. He searched everywhere, and each day felt like a hopeless attempt to find any trace of them.

He watched for her every day, hoping that he would spot her somewhere, but he couldn't think of any place where she might be. Every corner of the city felt unfamiliar, and no place seemed like the right one to look. His thoughts were scattered, and he couldn't find a direction to head in.

After days of searching, he remembered a location where they had met. It was a place that Viyaara had once told him about, saying that he should always come here if he needed to find her. The memory of her voice echoed in his mind, and he decided to go there, hoping for a chance to find some answers. Viyaan arrived there quickly, his heart pounding with both hope and fear.

As he stood there, something caught his eye—there was a **LETTER.**

His hands trembled as he picked it up and began to read it. His mind went blank as he processed the words on the paper. He was shocked and unable to speak. The emotions hit him all at once. He wasn't ready for what he had just read.

Instead of feeling relief or clarity, he erupted in rage, feeling overwhelmed by a mix of anger and sadness. The weight of everything finally broke' him, and he started crying. It was a moment he couldn't explain, but it felt like everything had come crashing down in an instant.

Without thinking, he immediately went home, packed his belongings, and hurried to buy a ticket. He left for a month's vacation, without telling anyone what had happened to him or why he was acting this way. As Viyaan hurried to the airport to board his flight back to India, he felt as if his life was about to change **AGAIN.**

The content of the letter was so shocking that Viyaan was unable to process it. He realized that he was soon going to see the...***THE LAST OF HER...***

CHAPTER FIVE

THE LAST OF HER

He read the letter, which stated, "I knew you liked me and you let go of me for the person I thought I liked but did I?. I acknowledge your change Viyaan you have become a person no one ever thought and I came London 2 years ago saw you here but was not confident to meet you so waited and I found an opportunity and strength to talk to you back so I came and I saw you like a completely different person I'm sorry I didnt tell you this that I couldnt propose to the guy because I have always loved you from bottom of my heart and I was lying to myself till that very moment and I always wanted you to see how much you have changed and the Viyaan I knew never cared truly for anyone But this viyaan knows how to control tears when they start to fall. I saw the tears, and I was so proud that you didn't think of yourself. You are the viyaan I always wanted, so don't change and yes why didnt I tell you that I love you becausse I'm going back to India why? because I'm dying yes you read it right . I've been fighting from Neurodegenerative disorder for four years doctors have given up now and to be honest I cant keep fighting even my heart is too weak now, but its still full of love and I didnt wanted you to know this because then you wouldnt be able to see how much changed you are. I've decided to pass away in India so everyone can see me there, especially you. I know you'll rush to India to see me, and then everyone will see the changed Viyaan. I'm delighted you'll be there to witness THE LAST OF ME, hahahaha."

When he arrived in India, he was surprised to see all of his society friends waiting to embrace him. He couldn't believe it. He had just received that shocking letter, and now he found himself surrounded by everyone he knew. He was unable to process everything that had just happened. Viyaan, once again, found himself at a loss for what to do. He felt overwhelmed, not knowing what the right step was.

His first question was, "Where is Viyaara?" His voice was filled with concern, as he looked around at his friends. Everyone gathered around and quickly replied. They told him that Viyaara wanted them to see his change, so she had returned. They explained that the man she had been dating was with her the entire time and wanted Viyaan to be there as well.

"The past is a four-letter word that will follow you around forever , It will resurface in ways you don't like, but you have to deal with it. It's part of life."

The past couldn't be erased, but he had changed. The person he was now was different from the one he used to be. He needed to accept that, just as Viyaara had. He went to his house, where he met everyone and Viyaara's parents. The atmosphere was a mix of sadness and hope. He could feel the weight of the situation in the air. Viyaara had wanted all of his friends to be together again, just like the good old days.

So, they all went somewhere and spent time together. They even took Viyaara along, and everyone watched a movie together. The laughter filled the room, and conversations flowed easily. Viyaan noticed that Viyaara looked happy the entire time. Despite everything, the group managed to create new memories, and for a little while, the sadness that hung over them seemed to lift.

It was a special time. All of them were on the edge of shedding tears, but they managed to stay strong for Viyaara. They knew she needed them, and they wanted to cheer her up. It was a bittersweet moment filled with both joy and sadness, but they all tried to keep their spirits up for her sake.

When it was time to take her back, Viyaan were the first to arrive. The moment felt strange to Viyaan, but he respected the situation. In an unbelievable turn of events, Viyaara's family, asked, **Viyaan to carry Viyaara in his arms.** It was a quiet, unspoken gesture, but Viyaan appreciated it deeply. He hadn't expected such a thing, but he knew it meant something so big.

Viyaara had about a month with her friends. During that time, they all did their best to make the journey successful. They kept her surrounded with love and support, making sure she never felt alone. Each day was filled with little acts of kindness, laughter, and memories they created together.

They lived beautifully in that time they had, knowing it was limited. They cherished every moment, and Viyaara felt a sense of belonging that she hadn't felt in a while. She didn't have to face the pain of loneliness. All of Viyaan's friends helped her feel like she was still part of the world she once knew.

Viyaara was grateful for their efforts, but there was a bittersweetness that lingered. Time was running out, and they all knew it. But they refused to let her feel sad. They wanted her to have the happiest days possible, even if the future was uncertain.

As each day passed, Viyaan realized how much he had changed. He had come a long way from the person he used to be. He was no longer the guy who took things for granted, who never thought about the consequences of his actions. Now, he understood the value of love, kindness, and friendship. And he was ready to face whatever came next, whether it was the past, the future, or something in between.

Viyaara's time with them was coming to an end, but the memories they had created would last a lifetime. They would never forget the way they came together in her final days, and how love and friendship helped them through the most difficult time.

Without wasting any time, Viyaan and Viyaara had their last conversation, where Viyaan said, **"You are really cruel. You called me here, as if everyone could see me, but you showed yourself to me in this condition. You know how much I think about you, and I will always think of you that way. I never knew that meeting you in London would make me fall in love with you that day, and now look at today, just the thought of you fills me with love. I'm not ready for this. I can't handle it. Please forgive me, I wasn't a good guy before, and maybe I'm still not. But I do know this that I will never be able to forget you because you're leaving a piece of yourself with me. And that piece is every last word of yours, which is now in my heart and mind. Please don't go, please don't leave."** on which Viyaara replied, **"Who is this Viyaan that I don't know? Who is this Viyaan who is stopping me and asking me not to go? Who is this Viyaan holding onto me? But whoever this Viyaan is, he is the most beautiful because he is mine. No one could have been a better friend to me than you,** and maybe no one ever will be. God is calling me, so I can become his friend. What can I do? I am really good. Please take care of yourself. I'll always be with you, in your memories."

All of Viyaan's friends came over and crowded him in for hugs as they rejoiced over his transformation, while he was crying alone and didn't want anyone to see. *You will lose your favourite individuals along the way in life, so you must be strong and remember all of your fond memories of them.* They hurried to the hospital to see her, but she was too unconscious to speak, and everyone broke down in tears. Viyaara asked for Viyaan. He went inside and saw a letter. It stated, **"Don't feel sad for my situation. I'm happy you're sitting beside me and reading this letter and seeing me, Viyaan. You were always the guy who connected with me, and I can trust you. I have no words of what to say in this situation. I had the strength to talk to my parents and my brothers and sisters, but I knew you needed to hear from me for the last time, so I wrote this letter. I wish you the best on your future journey. I'll always love you and cherish the moments you have given me. This *SOFT makhmali* nature of yours is the best. Please hug me and tell everyone you saw the last of me and that I will always love them."**

Everyone was crying except for Viyaan when he first phoned her parents and then her brothers and sisters, who knew she would always be strong, and that he needed to be strong too. It was a moment of deep emotion, but he held himself together.

"Ae khuda voh tere dar per aa rahi hai usko kabhi akela mat chodhna..."

He understood that sometimes, being strong doesn't mean not feeling the pain. It just means pushing through it with grace and dignity, knowing you have to keep going, even when life feels impossible. There were so many emotions swirling in his chest grief, fear, regret, love, and loss. But in that moment, he chose to stay composed. He knew that his strength would give others the strength they needed.

Viyaan knew that sometimes, life doesn't give you the luxury of falling apart. Sometimes, *life demands that you pick up the pieces and keep moving forward, no matter how heavy your heart feels*. He understood that, even though the world around him was breaking apart, he had to be the one to keep it all together for the people who needed him.

In the silence of the room, as everyone else shed their tears, Viyaan found a quiet kind of resolve. He understood that being strong didn't mean avoiding pain, it meant facing it head-on and continuing the journey, one step at a time.

When Viyaan left for London, he met everyone who mattered in his life one last time. They all gave him their best wishes and assured him that he would never be alone. It was their way of telling him that no matter where he went, they would always be with him in spirit.

It was a bittersweet farewell, but Viyaan was grateful for the love and support they had given him, especially during the hardest times of his life. It wasn't easy to say goodbye to people who had been there for him through thick and thin, but Viyaan knew it was time to move forward. He would carry their love with him, wherever he went.

But what made the farewell even more difficult was the realization that life had changed so much. When he first made the decision to leave, it had felt like the right thing to do. He was leaving behind the past, leaving behind the pain, and stepping into a future that seemed full of unknown possibilities.

But now, as he stood there saying his goodbyes, he couldn't ignore the weight of the memories. He had learned to let go of so many things, but saying goodbye to the people who had been his pillars was one of the hardest things he'd ever had to do.

Viyaan knew the importance of love, not just from what he had given, but also from the heartache he had experienced. He had lost the same person twice, but the difference this time was that he had changed. He had grown and learned.

He had become a different person because of the love he had for Viyaara, and because of the lessons he had learned from the pain he endured. He carried with him just one memory from India, the memory that he got to see **THE LAST OF HER**.

That memory was both beautiful and painful, a reminder of the time he had lost and the love he would never fully have. It was bittersweet, a memory that would stay with him forever.

He had learned that love doesn't always work out the way you expect. Sometimes, love leaves you with more pain than happiness. But even in that pain, there are lessons.

Love had taught Viyaan that sometimes you have to lose someone to realize just how much they meant to you. But this time, it wasn't just about the love he had lost, it was also about the love he had gained from the experiences that shaped him into who he was now.

The Viyaan who left India was a different person from the one who had arrived. And that change, that growth, was something he had earned through both joy and sorrow.

Each stage of life reminds you that people can change when they recognize their mistakes. Viyaan had made his share of mistakes, but he had finally realized the importance of admitting his own faults. It wasn't easy, but it was necessary for his own growth.

He had spent so much time avoiding his mistakes, covering them up with pride and denial. But now, after everything he had been through, he understood that growth wasn't possible without self-awareness. It wasn't about being perfect, but about acknowledging where you went wrong and striving to be better.

It wasn't easy to face the truth of his actions, but Viyaan understood that accepting his mistakes was the only way forward.

He had been afraid to admit his shortcomings, afraid of how others would see him. But now, he saw that accepting his mistakes didn't make him weak rather it made him stronger. It took strength to admit where he had gone wrong, and it took courage to try and make things right.

For the first time in his life, Viyaan wasn't running from his flaws. He was facing them head-on, determined to learn from them.

For Viyaan, love had transformed him into a person who could finally see the value of caring for someone else. He was no longer the same person he had been before.

His heart had grown, and he had learned to give and care in a way he never thought possible. It wasn't just about finding someone to love, it was about learning to love in a deeper, more meaningful way.

The love he had for Viyaara had changed him. It had made him realize that love wasn't something to take lightly. Love was about sacrifice, understanding, and being there for someone, no matter what.

For so long, Viyaan had been focused on what he could get out of a relationship. But love had taught him that the true value of love came from what you were willing to give, not take. He had learned that love was not a game, and it was certainly not something you should take for granted.

Viyaan had started to care for Viyaara not because he needed to, but because he wanted to. Love had taught him that it was worth it. Everyone has that one person in their life who will always be there, who will always support them, no matter what.

That person is your **MAKHMALI** *person—a soft person*, yet strong in ways you never expected. It's the kind of person you need in your life, the kind of person you should hold on to. Viyaan had found that in Viyaara. Despite everything that had happened, despite the pain and the heartbreak, he knew that she was the person who had shaped him into who he was today.

Love changes people, and it gives them the strength to face their own flaws, embrace their future, and move forward with hope.

Viyaan knew that he would always carry the lessons love had taught him. Even though he was far from perfect, love had made him someone who could face the future with hope, knowing that he was capable of being better, of loving better, and of living a life full of meaning.

Viyaan had been in London for weeks now, but there was something that kept pulling him back to the same place, again and again.

No one knew why he visited this particular spot so often. It seemed like a mystery to everyone around him. But Viyaan had his reasons, deep and personal reasons that no one could truly understand.

The truth was, this place was the key to the last piece of Viyaara—the **LETTER**. The letter was the last thing she left behind. *The last connection to her.*

It wasn't just a piece of paper with words on it. No, it was much more than that. It held **her essence**, her presence, her love. Whenever Viyaan went to that place, he could feel her near. It was as if the air itself carried her spirit, whispering memories of the love they once shared.

This place had become more than just a location for Viyaan; it had become a sanctuary, a space where his heart could feel at peace.

This spot in London was the place where everything had changed. It was where Viyaan had found the letter that would forever tie him to Viyaara. The letter wasn't just a message; it was a reflection of her thoughts, her emotions, and her *final words to him*.

Viyaan could never forget the way he had felt when he first read those words. The letter wasn't a goodbye, but a reminder of the love they had shared, and of all the moments they had together.

Every day, he would return to this place. It became his **MAKHMALI space**—a term that meant softness, comfort, and a place that reminded him of the gentleness of his own heart.

This place had a way of softening him, of reminding him of the kindness he once had, the softness that had been buried deep beneath his tough exterior.

There was a time when Viyaan had been proud of his ego. He had been a man who was driven by pride, and nothing could shake him. But Viyaara had changed him. *Her love had softened his heart* in ways he never thought possible.

Her gentle nature, her kindness, and the way she loved him without hesitation, had brought down the walls around his heart. It was as though her love had given him the strength to be vulnerable.

And now, this place—this quiet, peaceful corner of London—was where he would go every day to reflect, to remember, and to heal. It was his space, his retreat, where he could be soft and open to the memories of her. Here, the world would stop for a moment, and he would feel at peace with himself, knowing that he could love again without fear.

But the journey wasn't easy. Each day that Viyaan visited the spot, the pain of losing Viyaara crept back. It was like an old wound reopening, yet at the same time, it was a way of keeping her memory alive.

He had come to understand that grief was not something that could be easily forgotten. It was something that needed to be honored, something that needed to be felt, in order for him to move forward.

Viyaan would sit there, sometimes for hours, just staring at the spot where they had shared so many moments. Those moments, though small, were what had made his idea of love so special.

It wasn't about grand gestures or loud declarations; it was about the quiet moments in between, the subtle touches, the whispered words, and the shared smiles.

He often thought about the letter. It was more than just words on paper. It was the last part of Viyaara that he could hold on to. And that was why he kept coming back.

It was his way of keeping her close. The letter was a reminder of everything they had been through, and it would always remain a part of him.

In this space, Viyaan had learned to let go of his ego. The man who had once been so proud, so certain of himself, now understood the power of love and vulnerability.

Viyaan knew that his journey wasn't over. The letter, though precious, couldn't bring her back. But it was a part of him now, and in that sense, she would never truly be gone. Every time he visited his Makhmali space, he could feel her love surrounding him, filling him with the strength to continue on.

The Makhmali space would always hold the memories of Viyaara, and for as long as Viyaan lived, he would carry her love in his heart. The letter, the place, and the lessons he had learned would always remind him of the softness within himself and the power of love. And that, he knew, was the true essence of life.

"You may all have a place, a special ornament, a letter, the last text, a final photo, or many other precious things that hold memories of those you love. Remember to hold onto those moments tightly, for they are what make you a soft, compassionate person. God always takes care of the ones He loves, and when you choose to live with kindness and softness, you become someone who supports and nurtures others until the very end. Be that soft person. Be the one who offers comfort, love, and understanding, and never let go of the moments that remind you of the beauty in life and the people who touched your heart."

'REMEBER, LOVE COMES IN THE MOST UNEXPECTED WAYS AND HAS THE POWER TO CHANGE YOU FOREVER AND EVER'

Love Is To Let Go

"Usse mohabbat pehle kabhi hui nahi per jab hui tabh aese hui ki usse jaane dena he meri sabse badhi mohabaat ki nishani thi"

("I had never loved her before, but when I did, it was in such a way that letting her go became the biggest symbol of my love.")

Viyaan had never loved Viyaara before, but as the years went by, something changed. It wasn't until the day he saw her at the reception that he truly realized he had fallen in love with her. It's the kind of story you often hear, where you unexpectedly meet someone and, in that very moment, you fall in love. For Viyaan, that moment was real. But the most unexpected part of his love story wasn't how it started rather it was how it ended. Viyaan's greatest love came to an end not through distance or time, but by **letting her go**.

Time Never Waits

"Sahi waqt mai mohabbat ki kadar nahi kari toh jab meri mohabbat ki baari aayi waqt ne usse hee mujhse cheen liya"

("I didn't value love at the right time, then when it was my turn to be loved, time took it away from me.")

Viyaan didn't love Viyaara when she gave him her whole heart and life. She had always been there for him, offering everything she had. But when it finally became his turn to be loved, time took her away from him. She was no longer there, and Viyaan was left all alone, realizing too late the depth of his feelings for her.

They Will Be Always There

"Jaa chuke hai voh toh kya hua, apni mohabbat per aitbaar karna palat ke dekhoge toh aaj bhi vahi khade hai voh"

("Just because she has gone, what does it matter? Trust in your love, and if you look back, you'll still find it standing right there.")

Viyaara was gone, but Viyaan still had her memories, and he held onto them tightly. Even though she wasn't physically with him, he carried her in his heart every day. Throughout his life, he loved her, even without having her by his side. That's the beauty of trusting in your love that it doesn't always need to be with you to still have a powerful presence in your life. True love stays with you in your heart, no matter the distance.

Story Has Not Ended

"Agar tum miljaate toh kissa isse janam mai khatam hojaata lagta hai abh kissa lamba jaayega..."

("If I had met you, this story would have ended in this lifetime. But now, it seems the story will go on for much longer...")

Viyaan lost Viyaara, but maybe God had other plans. Maybe they were meant to keep the story alive in a different way, and they will meet again in another universe. So, when you lose someone, don't worry. There might be a bigger story to it, one that continues in ways you can't yet understand. Sometimes, what feels like an end could be the beginning of something new, somewhere else, at a different time.

Waited Your Entire Life

"Meri aakhien uska intezaar kar rahi thi per shayd bhagwan mujhse thoda zyadda kar rahe thee..."

("My eyes were waiting for her, but maybe God was waiting for her more than I was...")

Viyaan was waiting to see her every day, hoping for just one more moment with her. But God had a different plan, He wanted Viyaara with Him. Sometimes, when you lose someone, it's important to understand that maybe they were needed more elsewhere. Your story might have a different ending, one that you don't fully understand yet. So, when you lose someone, remember, it doesn't always mean they were meant to stay with you. Their journey was meant to go a different way.

In Her Memories

"Uski yaad mai aaj bhi kuch khushiyaa aur baatlunga, uski yaad mai aaj bhi muskura kar zindagi jee jaaunga, uski yaad mai aaj bhi agar kam padhe yeh zindagi toh ek janam aur jee jaaunga"

("In her memory, I will still find some happiness and speak about her. In her memory, I will continue to smile and live my life. And if this life isn't enough, I will live another one, all in her memory.")

You tend to live with their memory, carrying it with you in everything you do. You make sure that each moment, every action, is dedicated to them, as if they are a memory you never want to lose. And if this life feels too short, you would come back and live again, just to be in their memory once more. This was the kind of love Viyaan had for Viyaara. When he saw her again after four years, it wasn't just a reunion rather it was the rekindling of a love that had lived on in his heart, untouched by time, continuing to thrive in his memories.

Cover Page Relevence

The front cover depicts two people in love, bathed in the warmth of daylight and surrounded by a bright, beautiful sun and scenery. As time passes, the day fades, the sun sets, and with it, the light dims. By the time night falls, you find yourself standing alone, reflecting on what once was. This is the essence of our back cover — a story of love that, like the setting sun, eventually fades into the quiet solitude of night.

Extra

1. Story was originally written in november 2022 and that was of 21 pages.

2. The story inital title was choosen as "The last of her".

3. The climax was thought different but when I started writing in 2022 november I changed it.

4. Only 8 of my friends read the first 21 page story(Thankful to them)

Thank You

Thank you, readers, friends, and family, for reading this story. I'm sorry I'm not a professional writer, but I'm a storyteller. I tried to put the story in a way that you all can like and love.